THE NEW AGE

TARROK
THE BLOOD SPIKE

With special thanks to Troon Harrison

www.beastquest.co.uk

ORCHARD BOOKS
338 Euston Road, London NW1 3BH
Orchard Books Australia
Level 17/207 Kent St, Sydney, NSW 2000

A Paperback Original
First published in Great Britain in 2012

Beast Quest is a registered trademark of Beast Quest Limited
Series created by Beast Quest Limited, London

Text © Beast Quest Limited 2012
Inside illustrations by Pulsar Estudio (Beehive Illustration)
Cover by Steve Sims © Beast Quest Limited 2012

A CIP catalogue record for this book is available from
the British Library.

ISBN 978 1 40831 842 3

5 7 9 10 8 6 4

Printed and bound by CPI Group (UK) Ltd, Croydon, CR0 4YY

The paper and board used in this paperback are natural recyclable
products made from wood grown in sustainable forests. The
manufacturing processes conform to the environmental regulations of
the country of origin.

Orchard Books is a division of Hachette Children's Books,
an Hachette UK company

www.hachette.co.uk

Tarrok
The Blood Spike

BY ADAM BLADE

ORCHARD

Henkrall
FORESTED SINKHOLE
GREAT NORTHERN MARKET
GEYSER ISLAND

I heard of Avantia in my youth, when I flew with the other children over the plains of Henkrall. They said it was a land of beauty, bravery and honour. A place of noble Beasts, too.

Even then it made me sick.

I can't fly now. My cruel mistress, Kensa, was jealous of my wings, so she took them. Don't pity me, Avantians – it's you who should be afraid. Your time is coming. Kensa has plans for your green and pleasant land. Your Good Beasts will be no defence against her servants – they'll be powerless!

You'll need more than courage to protect you from the Beasts of Henkrall!

Your sworn enemy,

Igor

PROLOGUE

Cywen balanced on the cliff edge. Far below, desert dunes were purple in the dawn shadows. The breeze teased the edges of Cywen's wings as he spread them wide. He glanced around, making sure no one had noticed him leaving. The stone houses of Velora were silent on the plateau but soon cooking fires would be kindled. *I must leave now*, he thought.

He folded his arms over his chest, tucked his hunting spear against his body, and leaped off the cliff. Briefly he dropped, before finding an air current. His wings lifted him into the first sunlight. A worried frown creased Cywen's forehead. It was the third dawn since Efflyn had gone hunting and not returned. He swung in mid-air and headed towards the desert to search for his missing sister.

Perhaps she had got lost. Cywen knew this could easily happen. The sand shifted constantly, driven in the wind like waves. New dunes formed and old ones wore away, making the desert impossible to map.

The day before Efflyn disappeared, he remembered, she said something strange. Something about the sand moving. What was it? Oh yes, she said she'd seen the sand moving even though there was no breeze.

Cywen felt a chill along his wing feathers. What had Efflyn seen out there?

She wasn't the only one missing. Yesterday, two more hunters had failed to return to Valora.

Cywen flew on until the plateau became a distant smudge. The sun rose, a red disc. The tall green cacti cast long shadows. Cywen's shadow flapped amongst them. Nothing else moved except an occasional lizard.

There's nothing large enough out here to hurt me or Efflyn, Cywen reminded himself.

He was growing tired. He soared in a circle, resting his wings. Although he scanned the desert, he saw nothing that might lead him to Efflyn. No tracks, no broken spear or dropped water flask.

Swooping lower, he cried her name.

The only reply was the shriek of a bird. Cywen grew hotter as he came closer to the sand. *It's hopeless*, he thought. *Her water will all be gone, and no one can survive long in this heat...*

He wiped his brow, and noticed something ahead. A cloud! He narrowed his eyes and watched the cloud moving. Anxiety began to prickle across his skin.

"No," he murmured. "It isn't an ordinary cloud. It's a sandstorm!"

Cywen flapped with all his strength. Although he rose quickly into the sky, the storm moved faster. Sand lashed him, stinging like the tips of a thousand whips. In the roaring darkness, feathers were shredded from his wings. Sand filled his ears and eyes. Pain tore at his back as he was tossed over and over. His grasp

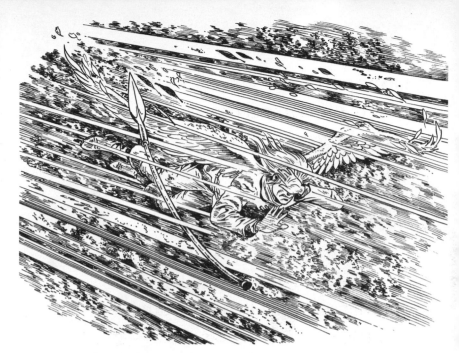

weakened on his spear, and wind
snatched it away.

*Perhaps this is what happened to Efflyn
and the others*, thought Cywen. *Now
they're dead beneath the sand.*

Cywen's stomach rose and plunged.
It was impossible to tell which direction
was up and which was down. Peering
through his fingers, he glimpsed a
chink of blue sky. Cywen beat his
wings in desperation, hoping to climb

above the storm and reach clear air.

Something tugged at his legs. Cwyen glanced down and saw dark swirling sand. Shadows. Something green and spiky – a cactus? Was he that close to the ground?

The cactus seemed to twist and clench like fingers, and Cywen's eyes bulged in horror. A giant hand – covered in warts and spikes – was wrapped around his leg!

As he was hauled lower, Cywen saw two glaring red eyes. In the bulbous cactus-head, the slash of a mouth gaped open. Yellow drool stretched between green lips lined with prickles.

A Beast! Cywen thought, faint with terror. In the village, people told stories about the Beasts of other kingdoms. Cywen had shuddered in the firelight, listening to these stories

on winter nights. Now he knew
there was no escape for him.

*This Beast has already killed my sister.
Now it will kill me.*

The hand dragged him lower still.
Cywen struggled harder to break
free. He only succeeded in driving the
spikes deeper into his own legs. Blood
trickled over his ankles.

*My homeland of Henkrall – is it doomed
too?*

CHAPTER ONE

ANGRY EYES

Tom stood beside Tempest as the
horse grazed the shoreline, and patted
the horse's strange purple coat.

"Do you miss Storm?" Elenna
asked, sitting in the grass.

"Yes, but I'm glad we left him
and Silver safely in Avantia."

It had been too dangerous for
Storm and Silver to travel along the
Lightning Path on this Quest. Tom

felt grateful that their new animal companions had already proven their loyalty.

Tempest lifted his head from the grass. Unfolding his wings, he flapped to a brighter patch of green halfway up the cliff.

"A flying horse," Elenna marvelled again. "Everything is really different here in Henkrall."

"Everything except the Beasts," Tom said. He gazed over the sea and shuddered as he remembered diving into its depths. There he had fought the sea Beast called Elko. Somehow, Kensa the witch had shaped this Beast from clay, and brought it to life with blood stolen from the Good Beasts of Avantia.

"The water's safe again now," Elenna reassured Tom. Her shaggy wolf, Spark, scratched at the underside of one wing and yawned. Elenna laughed. "Even Spark agrees."

"He's used to living in a peaceful kingdom," Tom said. "But Henkrall won't stay peaceful now that Kensa has shaped corrupted Beasts. You know how much harm they can do."

Elenna's smile died. Kensa's evil had already been brewing whilst Tom's father, Taladon, was being buried.

"You're right," Elenna said. "We can't rest here for long."

Tom scanned the sky over the lapping waves and the soaring cliff. He saw nothing more frightening than a flock of swallows.

"What are you looking for?" Elenna asked.

"That hunchbacked servant of Kensa's. He and his flying hog can easily spy on us from the sky."

"We should move on," Elenna said. "We're easy targets here on the shore."

She called Spark and balanced on a rock to mount the wolf. Her hands disappeared into his shaggy ruff as she clasped handfuls of hair. Tom hefted his shield. Was it his imagination or did it seem lighter without the tokens from Avantia's Good Beasts? All the precious tokens had disappeared when he travelled the Lightning Path to reach the kingdom of Henkrall.

When I defeated Elko, one token returned to my shield, he thought. He gazed in satisfaction at Sepron's fang nestled in its usual space. Five more tokens to regain. Five more Beasts to fight here. *And no help from Aduro or my father now.*

"Where should we go next?"
Elenna's voice broke into Tom's
thoughts.

He looked at the shield's surface.
A magical map of Henkrall began to
glow in golden lines. His finger traced
a path over the mountain peaks.
Beyond lay a great expanse of sand
with the name *Tarrok* written on it.

"A desert, and our next Beast!"
Tom said.

"We've fought Beasts in the sand before," Elenna replied. "Hopefully our experience will pay off. Let's go!"

Tom whistled and Tempest cruised down from the cliff. His purple feathers and black mane glowed in the sparkle of the waves. Tom stroked the horse's nose before springing onto his back and nudging him into flight. Beside him, Elenna's wolf spread his wings, loped along the beach to gain speed, and launched himself after the horse. Tom whooped as the cliff soared past.

"This must be like riding Ferno!" Tom called.

"Better!" Elenna yelled back. "This time, you're not preparing to die under Malvel's blade."

But this time, I am facing the evil of a new witch, Tom thought. *At least with*

Malvel I knew what to expect.

Spark howled with delight as the creatures soared over the mountains in the soft breeze. Between the peaks lay rich forests, green valleys, and bright pastures. Once they swooped over a flock of sheep that scattered in alarm, half unfolding their woolly wings. In another pasture, young calves practised their flying skills from a rock. Their mother cows mooed encouragement to the timid ones scared to try their first flight.

"Look ahead!" Tom shouted. He pointed to a high range of mountains running across the horizon. "The desert should lie beyond that."

"We'll get there quickly at this speed," Elenna replied. Tom could see her eyes sparkling with the thrill of the ride.

The mountain range loomed closer, mottled with trees. A dark shadow rushed over the slopes. Tom glanced higher in surprise.

"A storm cloud?" he called to Elenna. The cloud swirled. Uneasily, Tom remembered the storm of thunder and lightning that he and Elenna had used to travel to Henkrall. He hoped this storm would not unleash its power onto them.

Elenna motioned upwards, and Tom nudged at Tempest. The horse and the wolf flapped hard, climbing higher to pass above the cloud. Chilly air rushed through Tom's tunic. He shivered and wondered how high the animals were able to go. Would they still be able to fly in this thin air?

But no matter how high they went, the cloud seemed to rise up too.

Tom patted Tempest's neck as the horse's wings heaved. Things moved up and down inside the cloud. *It's not a cloud at all*, Tom realized. *It's a flock of birds!* Their black bodies soared in close formation. Hundreds of pairs of wings screeched up and down, flapping fast but with a grinding noise. Sharp, shining beaks clacked angrily. They sounded like pieces of wood being smacked together.

One bird broke away from the rest and darted straight at Tom. He pulled Tempest's head sideways, making the horse fall through the air. Crouched low over Tempest's neck, Tom heard the bird screech past his shoulder, barely missing him. Two more birds shot from the flock, aimed at Tom. He dodged one of them, the horse bucking in the air. Tom raised his

shield and the other bird thumped
against it with a heavy, metallic clang.
In the corner of Tom's eyes, the bird
spiralled towards the ground far
below, one wing spinning loose.

A shock ran through Tom. *They're
not real birds!* He squinted at the
flock, now swirling upwards around
him and Elenna. Each bird was a
mechanical contraption, formed

of wood and metal, painted black. But what evil magic had given them the power of flight?

Before he could ask Elenna, the entire flock swerved and changed direction. The strange birds were heading straight towards them!

CHAPTER TWO

AERIAL BATTLE

Tom cried out as the birds swooped
around him. Sharp beaks jabbed at
his shoulders and back, shredding his
tunic and scratching his skin. Claws
scrabbled in his hair. Wings beat across
his face, blinding him. The cries of the
birds mingled with Elenna's screams,
Spark's howling, and Tempest's shrill
neigh. The horse pitched in the air.
Tom gripped as hard as he could with

his legs. What if he was thrown off
and fell to his death on the mountains
below? *I can't let that happen. I have
a Quest to complete!*

"Get away from me!" Elenna
shrieked as an especially large bird
sank its talons into her shoulder. Spark
lunged at the birds, his jaws snapping.

"We need to head downwards and
try to escape!" Tom called.

He nudged Tempest behind the front legs. Immediately the horse pitched into a dive, dodging from side to side. Tom wrapped his hands in his mane and held on. Birds thumped against his head and shoulders. Blood trickled down his arms. A beak slashed across his cheek.

The birds have been sent by Kensa, Tom realized. *They are half-constructed, half-magical.*

Tempest neighed in pain, but at that moment they tumbled out from the bottom of the flock. Feathers drifted around as the ragged flock swirled across the sky. Tom glanced back to make sure that Elenna was still following. Her face was scratched and bleeding. Tufts of hair were missing from Spark's shoulders.

"Hang on tight!" Tom shouted, but at

that moment, Tempest pitched sideways. Tom was tossed into the air, his hands wrenching at the mane. He landed back on the horse with a thump that knocked his breath out. Still Tempest rocked and shuddered as he flew. Tom glanced at the horse's wings and saw that one was torn and bleeding.

"The birds have injured Tempest!" Tom shouted. "We have to find somewhere to land!"

He peered down, expecting to see forests and meadows. Instead, they were flying over a wide plateau that formed a flat place in the mountains. Along its edges, the plateau fell away in steep rocky cliffs. The plateau was covered in huge – nests? Tom squinted at the dark piles of sticks. He realized that he was looking at a mountain village. The grey stone buildings were pressed together along the cliff edge and others were built into the side of the cliff. More rose from spires of rock. The buildings' roofs were made from bundles of dark branches.

"Maybe we can land in the square!" Elenna pointed to an open place in the heart of the buildings.

"Let's try," Tom replied, but he was worried about Tempest. The horse's head drooped with pain, and his wing beats were growing weak. He couldn't keep airborne for much longer.

"Come on, boy, keep going a little further!" Tom said. They fluttered down in jerky movements.

The mountain loomed closer. It was terraced with with fields shaped like narrow strips and surrounded by stone walls. Crops filled each field. The tops of fruit trees almost brushed Tom's toes as

Tempest struggled to fly. *We're not going to make it!*

"Jump off Tempest and join me," Elenna suggested, flying alongside. Tom glanced sideways at Spark's wide, panting mouth and Elenna's outstretched arm.

"I can't abandon him," he said. "And I don't think Spark can carry us both. I'm going to try landing in that field ahead."

He turned Tempest towards a long terrace that waved with bright grass. The horse pitched and swooped. His hooves clattered across a wall. He snorted in alarm, and Tom lurched against his neck. Then the green grass rushed up like a wave. Tom flew headfirst into it, everything whirling around him. A blow shuddered through Tom's head.

Then everything went dark.

"Wh... What happened?" Tom
struggled to sit up. His mouth was
dry, and pain throbbed in his head.
He tried to focus his eyes. All he
could see were grey stones piled on
top of each other. Tom groaned and
clutched his aching shoulder. *Tempest?
Elenna? Where am I?*

Tom reached out and felt a rough

blanket beneath his fingers. "Hello?" he said.

Suddenly Elenna was beside him, looking pale. She squeezed his hands. "Tom," she said softly, "I've been so worried about you. Please lie still. You've hit your head."

"The Quest..." Tom groaned, clutching at the blanket and trying to make his legs move. He didn't have time to lie around while Kensa was wreaking her magic on Henkrall. Who knew what devastation her Beasts might spread? And if they found a way to rip portals to Avantia...

"Lie still," Elenna repeated. "You need to feel better before you worry about fighting any more Beasts."

Tom turned his aching head. The stones were the walls of a room, he could see now. On three sides there

were no windows but in the fourth
wall was an open doorway filled
with blue sky.

"Where are we?" Tom asked.

Elenna's mouth tightened. "We
were brought here after the crash.
I'm fine, and the people of the village
bandaged your head, Tom. They
didn't seem unkind. They've taken
the animals away and said they
would care for them."

"Then what's the problem?" Tom
asked. "We can leave."

He struggled to sit up but something
cut into his wrists. He wondered if his
arms were injured. Then he saw the
thick ropes knotted around his wrists
and around the bed frame. He looked
back up at his friend. Her eyes were
clouded with trouble.

"We're prisoners here," Elenna told him.

CHAPTER THREE

A PRISON WITHOUT LOCKS

"Prisoners?" Pain shot through Tom's head. "Where is my sword? Can't you cut me free with it?"

"The people took your sword and your shield," Elenna said. "And they took my arrows too." She gestured to where her quiver lay in a corner of the room.

Tom stared all around the room

but it was empty except for the bed
where he was tied.

"Is your quiver completely empty?"
Tom asked. "Don't you keep a spare
arrowhead?"

"You're right!" Elenna lifted the
quiver and rummaged inside. After a
moment she pulled out an arrowhead
and sawed its flinty edges across
Tom's ropes. Gradually it cut through

the tough fibre. When the ropes fell off, Elenna rubbed circulation back into Tom's wrists.

"Thank you," he said, staggering to his feet. His stomach lurched and for a moment he thought he would be sick. Then his dizzy vision settled and he took a deep breath.

"Who has imprisoned us?" he asked.

Elenna hung her head and shrugged. "I don't know," she said. "Flying people of Henkrall. There were too many for me to fight alone. I'm sorry, Tom. I've let us down. I should have protected you when you were injured."

"No, I'm the one who let us down. If only I'd kept Tempest in the air for another few moments, I could have landed him safely on the terrace."

He stared at the open doorway which let in sunlight. Unsteady but determined, Tom marched toward it.

"No, Tom, don't!" Elenna cried.

"I'm going to get my sword and shield, then find Kensa's next Beast," Tom said without looking back. "The Quest will go on!"

He lurched to the doorway. His arms wheeled wildly around his head. His mouth gaped in shock. There was no village street outside the door – they were on a cliff edge. Outside was nothing but empty air. Hundreds of feet below, sand gathered at the base of the cliff.

Tom heard Elenna's quick footsteps. She grabbed his shoulder and pulled him back into the room.

"We're near the edge of the plateau that we saw from the air," she explained. "This building is on top of a rocky outcrop. There's a sheer drop all around us. For a flying person, it's no problem to come and go. But for us, this is a prison, even if we we're not tied up."

"We have to escape as soon as possible," Tom said. "The people of Henkrall don't know that danger is threatening their peaceful kingdom. I won't let the Evil Beasts bring destruction to this land."

"I tried to explain to them," Elenna said, dropping her arrowhead back into her quiver.

"Who are these people? Where is this place?" Tom wondered, still pacing up and down.

A flutter of wings and a rush of air made Tom and Elenna turn and look toward the doorway. An old woman blocked the light as she entered, folding her wrinkled wings. A younger man followed her, stocky against the blue sky, his face cruel and hard.

"You are in Velora," the old woman said, smoothing a stray feather into place.

"And you're being held on charges of murder," said the young man.

"Murder?" Tom said.

"What do you mean?" said Elenna.

"I am the Elder. My name is Pendor," explained the woman. "My companion is Harth. Four of our tribe have gone missing, hunting in the desert, over the last few days. First to disappear was a girl called Efflyn, then two boys – my own nephews. Finally, Efflyn's brother, Cywen, has vanished."

"We had nothing to do with this!"
Tom said, locking his gaze with
Harth's cold stare.

Harth snorted. "Nothing to do with
it? It can't be a coincidence that you
strangers are hanging around and our
tribes-folk go missing."

Tom swung to face Elenna. "It's the
Beast!" he said. "It lurks somewhere

in the desert near—"

"We have a witness, too!" Harth interrupted. "A traveller has told us that the two of you attacked him."

Elenna narrowed her eyes in suspicion. "What traveller? What are you talking about?"

"A poor, one-eyed hunchback called Igor," said Harth.

"It was Igor who attacked us!" Tom protested. "He's a liar who works for our enemy, and the enemy of all Henkrall: the witch called Kensa."

The old woman's face went pale as Tom spoke this name. Her wings twitched nervously. "Kensa?" she muttered doubtfully. "I thought the witch left our lands long ago."

"No, she is plotting to take over all of Henkrall," said Tom. He explained about the clay Beasts being brought to magic life through the blood stolen from Avantia's Good Beasts. The old woman listened attentively, but Harth folded his arms over his chest. Tom ignored the man's sneer and turned all his attention onto Pendor. If she was an Elder, maybe she had more wisdom.

"Pendor, I beg you to let us go now," Tom said. "Surely you can understand that the Evil Beasts will bring great destruction. I have seen this before with my own eyes. We must continue on our Quest."

"It's too late for that," Pendor said.

"She's right," Harth said. "The Veloran Council has already tried your case. You have been sentenced to death!"

CHAPTER FOUR

THE COUNCIL'S VERDICT

Tom held his gaze level with Harth's. "You're making a terrible mistake," he said. He tried to keep his voice calm, remembering how Aduro and King Hugo talked in the council chambers of Avantia. Those brave men did not betray their fear and neither did his father, Taladon.

"The evil that will sweep Velora

is worse than anything you can imagine," Tom continued. "We are the only people who can stop it."

Pendor nodded weakly, her shoulders sagging and her wings twitching again. Confusion clouded her eyes. Harth continued to glare at Tom with his mouth twisted in a sneer.

"You're the only ones who can stop it?" he said. "You think a lot of yourselves."

Elenna glared at him. "In our kingdom of Avantia, Tom is a Master of the Beasts. You shouldn't mock things that you don't understand."

"You're a feisty one—" Harth started, but Pendor hushed him with a wave of her hand.

"We will fly back to the Veloran Council and tell them your story," she said. Her wings partially unfolded before she jumped out the doorway. Harth shot a final glare over his broad shoulders. "Make sure to stay here until we come back," he said. Then he jumped out and spread his wings to soar off into the blue sky.

Tom's legs began to shake. He backed against a wall and slid down it to crouch on the dirt floor. His head slumped into his hands as another wave of dizziness made the room spin. *Even if we get out of here, I won't be able to fight a Beast until my head mends. And how long will that take?* he thought.

Elenna sat beside him, leaning her shoulder against his. "A short rest will help you feel stronger," she said.

"Yes, but it's going to take more than a rest to make this situation better. We could be dead soon."

"I wonder how the Velorans kill their prisoners," Elenna said.

"Don't think about it. If only I had my shield, we could fly out of here." Tom shook his head miserably. "No, that's not true. Arcta's feather is missing from my shield, so we still couldn't fly."

"Flying didn't seem to help the missing Velorans. They must be victims of Kensa's new Beast."

Tom shuddered as another wave of dizziness rushed through his head. "We have to stop Tarrok, whatever he is," he said.

"Look!" said Elenna in surprise, and Tom opened his eyes.

Against the grey stones, a familiar face shimmered in a faint vision.

"Aduro!" Tom whispered. The good wizard's eyes twinkled and for a moment his beard twitched around his smile. Then his face became serious.

"Be brave," he urged. "I cannot help you with magic but you must stay strong. Think how terrible it will be if Kensa succeeds. Pursue your Quest. Avantia has faith in you!" The Wizard's voice and his image faded.

Tom hauled himself straighter against the wall. "Aduro is right," he

said. "While there's blood in my veins, I won't give up. "

"Nor will I," Elenna vowed. "Listen!"

With a soft rustle of wings, Pendor landed on the sill, weighted down with Tom's shield and sword, and with Elenna's bow and arrows.

"No time for discussion. We must be quick," she whispered, entering the room. "Harth will soon return with other men to take you away."

Tom leapt to his feet and reached for the weapons. It felt wonderful to hold his sword again. Elenna swung her bow over her shoulder with a smile.

"You must have believed us," Tom said.

Pendor ignored him as she laid a rectangular case onto the floor

and opened its lid.

Tom leaned over the case and saw
contraptions made from narrow
wooden struts and folded leather.
Pendor lifted one out. As she
unfolded it, Tom saw it was like
the wings of a bat.

"Our youngsters use these to learn

to fly, before their own wings are fully grown," Pendor explained.

"We – we can use them?" Tom asked doubtfully.

The wrinkles on Pendor's face deepened. "I hope so. It's the only thing I can think of to set you free. Quick, strap this around each shoulder."

Tom bent over as the old woman fastened the wings to his back, buckling the leather harness tight. He fiddled with the wings as Pendor fixed the other pair onto Elenna. *They seem too small and flimsy for us*, he thought.

"Are you sure this will work?" Elenna asked.

Pendor shrugged. "It's your only chance. Your animals are locked up and I can't get to them. They will be safe until you return. And if you never come back, I'll make sure they're cared for."

Tom and Elenna shot each other a doubtful look. Without their animal companions, could their Quest succeed in this land of flying creatures?

"Be brave," Tom said, stepping into the doorway. Space yawned beneath him. Far below, the desert was a sweep of pale gold. Tom sucked in a deep breath as Elenna stepped beside him. "Ready?" he said. "Now!"

Together, they jumped into the void.

Tom plunged down, arms wide. Wind whistled past his ears and his head spun. He jerked and flapped his arms, pushing against the rush of air.

But still he fell.

We're going to be bashed to death on the rocks below, he thought.

Maybe Pendor had tricked them

and this was how the Council killed its prisoners...

Elenna's scream filled his ears as the ground rushed closer.

CHAPTER FIVE

HEATSTROKE

Tom continued to flap desperately.
Just above the rocks, his fall slowed
down. He swooped sideways. A warm
draught of rising air filled his wings.
The leather stretched taut. He held
his arms level and worked them
smoothly up and down. Wobbling
slightly, he began rising up the face
of the cliff.

He glanced around for Elenna. She

was rising too, sometimes flapping and sometimes holding her wings still and gliding. "We're flying!" he whooped.

"Watch where you're going!" Elenna called and Tom's head swivelled. Just in time, he wobbled his wings. The tip of one brushed against the cliff. Tom slipped through the air in a slow spin. He flapped in a panic and regained smooth flight again. Turning in his harness, he shifted his weight and wobbled further away from the rocks, then rose higher in a wide swoop.

"This is incredible," Elenna called as she swung past Tom.

"I could do this all day!" Tom replied. The sun soothed his scratched arms and aching shoulders. He stared into birds' nests, and then

he soared away from the plateau,
heading over the rippled dunes of the
desert. Elenna followed. Their boots
whooshed over tall cacti and above
purple shadows and red rocks.

As time wore on, the heat grew stronger until Tom was sweating. Finally he glanced back. The plateau lay far behind, a tiny dot on the horizon.

"My arms are going to drop off," Elenna called.

Tom nodded. His arms were tired too and his wings creaked. He didn't think they could carry his weight for much longer. He tipped his wings and glided downwards. Dunes rushed to meet his feet. With a thump, his boots landed in a shower of sand.

When Elenna landed too, they unbuckled each other's harnesses. "I guess we'll have to leave these behind," she said.

"We don't want to carry anything extra in this heat," Tom agreed. "And we need to see if we can find the Beast."

He pulled his shield off his shoulder and checked the map on its surface. The golden lines glowed brightly as Tom traced them with his fingers. "We're near to the Beast now."

"Whatever it is," Elenna said, gazing around.

Tom tensed. For all they knew, Tarrok could be very close by, and they didn't know what he looked like.

They began to walk warily, scanning the landscape as they trudged up and over the peaked waves of the dunes. Coarse sand dragged at their footsteps. The sun climbed, beating down hotter and brighter, and their shadows shrank to nothing. Sometimes when Tom scanned the horizon, dizzy dots swung in his vision. Occasional pains darted through his head. *I hope I'll be strong enough for whatever awaits us. If only I could have a drink, I'd feel better. But my flask is in Tempest's saddlebag,* he thought.

A teasing wind sprang up. It lifted sand into the air and dropped it over Tom and Elenna. The grains stuck to their sweating skin. Tom's mouth was so dry that he had no spit left, not even enough to swallow with. His lips felt glued together, and his tunic was plastered to his wet back. Everything around him was turning into a golden haze.

And there – a golden figure. A man standing on a dune!

Tom paused and shaded his eyes.

Elenna bumped into him from behind. "What is it?" she asked.

Tom cleared the sand from his

throat. "Can't you see him? Who is he?"

Elenna squinted into the shimmering glare. "I don't see anyone at all."

"He's wearing armour," Tom muttered. Taladon? "Father!" Tom squeezed the word between his dry lips.

He staggered faster, kicking up sand, but the golden figure moved away, always just ahead. Tom began to run, a strangled cry breaking from his burning mouth. The figure was definitely Taladon, with his clear eyes under a lifted visor, his tall body, and his golden beard. A sob broke from Tom. He pounded up the next dune, his head throbbing, but again the knight had moved on. His armour was a golden haze on the next dune.

This makes no sense, Tom thought. *My father is dead. I'll never see him again.*

Grief squeezed Tom's chest.

"Tom, slow down!" Elenna called faintly from behind.

Tom's gaze was fixed on the knight. The sun sparkled on his helmet. Suddenly the figure dissolved into the heat haze. Tom blinked and pressed a hand to his pounding forehead.

Not my father. Just a mirage. I need to keep calm. He took a deep breath of scorching air. Swinging around, he waited as Elenna struggling up the dune, panting.

She gave him a concerned look. "Are you alright?" she asked.

"I'm fine. I must have been hallucinating. Let's stay focused on finding the Beast."

Swivelling to look ahead, Tom gasped. Hundreds of men in green uniforms stood at attention in the desert. "An army!" Tom squinted into the glare. When he shook his head, his vision cleared. He grinned.

"Not an army," he said. "Just cacti."

"I can see them too," Elenna agreed. "They're real."

"And real cacti hold real water!" Tom said triumphantly.

The tip of Elenna's tongue moved over her peeling lips. "What are we waiting for?"

Tom rushed down the slope, drawing his sword. He hacked at the first cactus he reached. It broke with a juicy sound. Water oozed from the cut, almost as thick as jelly. Tom speared the broken cactus on his sword and hefted it overhead, letting water drip into Elenna's mouth. She made a face as it hit her tongue. When Tom had his turn to drink, he grimaced too – the water was stale and hot.

"It's better than nothing," said Elenna, wiping her mouth on her sleeve.

"And it might have saved our lives," Tom said. He tensed as something moved behind Elenna's shoulder.

Something lying in the sand…
There was the outline of a body and then, above the sand, an arm waving. Flipping the broken cactus off the tip of his sword, Tom held the blade steady. Elenna whirled to follow his gaze.

"What is it? Is it the Beast?" she whispered.

"It's a…man, I think," Tom said. "A man buried in sand!"

CHAPTER SIX

SEARCHING FOR THE BEAST

Still brandishing his sword, Tom strode towards the figure. At his side, Elenna notched an arrow to her bow. They bent warily over the buried body. Was this another mirage? No, the man was solid and real, with sand matted in his fair eyebrows. His hair, clothing and tattered wings were sifted full of sand.

The man squinted at them, moaning in pain.

"One of his wings is broken!" Elenna exclaimed.

"I don't think he's any threat," Tom said, sheathing his sword. He slid a hand beneath the man's shoulders and gently helped him to sit. Elenna sliced a piece off a cactus with an arrow, cradled the man's head, and

dripped the juice into his mouth. He coughed and spluttered.

"Thank you, strangers," he rasped. "You saved my life. But where are your wings?"

"We are from the kingdom of Avantia," said Tom. "We don't have wings. I am Tom and this is Elenna. What happened to you?"

The man coughed again and spat out sand. "My name is Cywen. I was searching for my sister who disappeared in the desert three days ago. I was hit by a sandstorm and then I was attacked by...something." Cywen's brow furrowed. "I smashed into the ground and crawled among the cacti to hide. Have you seen my sister?" His eyes blazed with brief hope but Tom could only shake his head.

"Sorry, friend," he said. "We're looking for whatever attacked you. We think it's an Evil Beast and when we find it, maybe we'll find your sister too."

"Beasts!" Cywen said. "In Henkrall?"

Tom quickly told him about Kensa and her plot to take over the kingdoms.

Cywen looked horrified. "If we find my sister, she'll be dead then, not alive."

"You survived, so maybe she did too," Elenna comforted him. Tom searched through the pockets in his belt and pulled out the green jewel of Skor.

"I have something that will help to heal you," he explained. Gently he spread Cywen's wing across his shoulders, running the crystal over the broken bones. Cywen's face contorted with pain but then relaxed as the emerald's magic healed him. The bones knitted back together and the feathers grew long and straight again.

"Incredible!" he gasped. "Are you a wizard?"

"No," Tom replied. "In my home kingdom of Avantia, my father was the Master of the Beasts."

"You would be welcome in my city of Velora," Cywen said.

Tom and Elenna glanced at each other with raised brows.

"We've already been in Velora," Tom said. "We had a misunderstanding with a man named Harth. We barely escaped with our lives and now we are wanted as fugitives."

Cywen snorted, flexing his wings. "Harth! That man's brain is the size of a bat dropping and his voice is as loud as thunder. He forces people to listen to him."

"He certainly does," said Elenna. "We are trying to save your kingdom from evil but no one in Velora would listen to our warnings."

"We need to keep moving," Tom said. "Will you come with us?"

Cywen struggled to rise but lurched with weakness. Tom and Elenna supported him by the arms until he gained his balance. "Thank you," he said. "We seem to be seeking the same thing, so I'll come with you."

Under the blazing sun, they struggled on, occasionally stopping to rest in the shade of a tall cactus or to drink more water.

"Look at this!" Elenna exclaimed. Cywen and Tom huddled around as she bent over something on the ground.

"It's a Veloran hunting spear," Cywen said, hefting the metal shaft. "Look for tracks."

But the wind had scoured the sand smooth, and no tracks were visible anywhere as they trudged along past occasional rocky outcrops.

After some time had passed, Cywen stopped again and bent over. "A whistle!" he exclaimed, picking a bone instrument up from the base of a cactus. "Velorans use whistles to raise an alarm in time of danger."

"At least we know your people came this way," Tom told Cywen, scanning the horizon. Nothing but sand and sky and cacti. *Where is the*

Beast? Was my shield map wrong?

Tom pulled his shield from his back and looked at the map's golden lines.

"Where do you think we are?" Elenna asked.

"We seem to be right in the centre of the desert," Tom replied, pointing. "See, here is the name of the Beast: *Tarrok.*"

"It looks as though we're very close to him."

"Yes," Tom agreed. "We're just about on top of him according to the map. So why can't we see him?"

Looking up from his shield, Tom gazed around. A few paces away, a warty cactus threw a long shadow in the afternoon sunlight. The shadow stretched almost to Tom's boots. He looked at the cactus in surprise. *Was it this close before? Why didn't I notice it?* The plant was deep green and covered in thick, golden spikes with points as deadly as spearheads.

Suddenly the plant moved, its top swaying…

"Watch out!" Tom shouted and grabbed his sword.

CHAPTER SEVEN

BODIES IN THE SAND

Sand sprayed into the air as the cactus thrust itself out of the ground. Tom's eyes bulged in shock. It was like watching a plant grow at super-speed. *This is not an ordinary desert plant!*

Tom unsheathed his sword blade, levelling the tip at the cactus as it continued to rise out of the dune. A giant hand emerged, bright green and covered in spikes. Each knuckle was bigger than Tom's head.

"Tarrok?" Elenna asked, pulling her bow from her shoulder.

"It must be! Get ready to fight!" Tom said. Cywen crouched behind him, clutching his spear.

The huge hand rose into the air on a long, prickly arm. A massive body emerged in a whirl of sand. It towered above them, ridged with bright green warts, its golden spines shining. Tom's heart hammered. The Beast's enormous chest was wider than a house. His head was bulbous like the top of a cactus. In his flat face, his cheeks were lined with spikes. Hairy prickles surrounded flat green lips. Two red eyes swivelled around. They fixed Tom with a glare.

Where's his weak point? Tom wondered.

He scanned Tarrok as the shower
of sand settled and he could see
the Beast clearly. On his vast chest,
his leathery skin seemed thinner.

Beneath it, Tom could make out the faint pulsing outline of a black heart, about the size of a man's head. *Elko's weakness was his heart*, Tom thought. *Perhaps this Beast is the same. But how will I get close enough to his chest?*

The Beast lurched forwards, roaring. His legs were as thick as tree trunks, his arms swung like massive clubs and drool hung from his lips.

"Move back, get away!" Tom shouted to Elenna and Cywen. He stood still, and kept his sword pointed at the advancing Beast's heart.

Tarrok puffed out his chest, and the spikes along his ribs and down his arms stood straight out like lance-points. He swung an arm towards Tom who parried the blow with his sword, but staggered back under the impact. Sparks flew off his blade as

the prickly spikes ran along its edge.
Tom winced as ringing filled his ears.
The Beast advanced again, crashing
his spiked limbs into the sand.

One wrong move and I'll be impaled,
Tom thought. *Run through with a spike.*

Tarrok paused and drew himself to
full height. Tom clenched his sword
and waited for the Beast's next move.
After sucking in a deep breath, the
Beast opened his mouth. A blast of
scorching air and whirling sand shot
out. It drove Tom backwards. From
the corner of his eye, he saw his
companions stagger for balance.

Tom pressed his lips shut, trying
not to breathe in. His eyes filled with
sand. Blinded, blinking madly, he
listened for the Beast's heavy stride.
Was he coming closer? Tom hefted
his shield up and peered around

it through slitted eyes. The Beast
towered before him. Then Tarrok
blasted Tom harder, punching him
with an almost solid wall of hot sand.
Tom somersaulted off his feet in the
blast. Legs and arms whirling, he

tumbled amongst the cacti and landed hard against something solid.

Elenna cried out and Tom realised that he'd been blown up against her and Cywen. They were huddled beside a rock.

"I'm sorry, did I hurt you?" Tom gasped as he struggled to sit up.

"I'm fine," Elenna said, rising to her feet.

Searching for his dropped sword, Tom felt something smooth. Smooth and wide and flat. Not his sword. Tom pulled the sand away from whatever lay beneath it.

"A face!" he gasped in shock.

"Efflyn!" cried Cywen, bending over the sheet of strange, glassy material. Beneath the surface, a girl's face stared up, twisted in terror.

"She's dead!" Cywen sobbed, on

his knees and scrabbling at the sand.
"The Beast got her!"

Elenna and Tom began to dig
too. Quickly they uncovered three
enormous transparent orbs. In each
one, frozen Velorans huddled in
poses of panic, their eyes round
with horror. Their wings were raised
above their backs, as if to protect
themselves.

"How has Tarrok done this?" said Elenna, patting Cywen's back as he rocked to and fro on his knees.

He pressed his hands to the hard material over his sister's head. Her hair shone behind the yellow wall.

"We must stop this cruel Beast!" Tom declared. He spotted his sword lying alongside the tombs and hefted it into the air. Spinning around, he saw the Beast amongst the cacti, lurching towards them.

Tarrok's red eyes burned like coals in the haze. His lipless mouth drooled strings of sticky sand.

"The Blood Spike has found you," he roared. "There's no escape now!"

CHAPTER EIGHT

A BLACK HEART

"While there's blood in my veins, I will stop your evil actions!" Tom yelled. He gritted his teeth as the Beast's shadow plunged him into gloom. He ducked beneath the whistling arms and their lethal spikes. Swinging his sword upwards, Tom dodged around Tarrok's legs. The desert heat pounded from every side, and sweat poured from Tom's

forehead and into his eyes. His hand
slipped on the hilt of his sword. He
tightened his grip and swung around
to attack the Beast again. This time,
he aimed for Tarrok's thick knees.
He was forced to dodge back as the
lumbering mass of warts and prickles
crashed an arm down. *He's faster than
he looks*, Tom thought.

Tom hacked at the spikes on
Tarrok's legs and lower arms, and
managed to knock a few off. They

sparked against his sword, and flew through the air like spears to jab into the sand. One raked across Tom's shoulder, ripping his tunic. *Any closer, and I would have been sliced open,* he thought. *These spikes are stopping me from getting near enough to Tarrok to wound him.*

Tom swung his sword at Tarrok's knees again, holding the hilt with both hands, his muscles straining. When Tarrok roared, sandy drool splattered Tom's head. There was no time to wipe it away. Tom leapt over a rock as Tarrok swiped at him. One of Elenna's arrows thrummed past Tom's head.

If I can't defeat this Beast, he'll rip open a portal to Avantia. Once again, my home will be threatened with destruction...

Tom glanced up at the whoosh

of wings. Cywen flew overhead,
clutching his spear.

"Aim for the Beast's heart!"
Tom shouted.

Cywen drew back his spear and
flung it. Tarrok batted it aside as if it
was a twig. The Veloran swooped to
recover it, his wings brushing the tops
of the cacti, his face white with terror.

*The winged man is doing his best
to help us*, Tom thought. *But he has
no experience of combat. Henkrall is a
peaceful kingdom.*

Tom fought on, hoping to wound
Tarrok in the knees and cripple him.
But he had no success, because he
was unable to get close enough as the
Beast rained blows with his arms.

Elenna was faring better. Her aim
was accurate, and each arrow she
shot embedded itself in Tarrok's warty

skin. The Beast roared, clawing at the arrows. Suddenly, one hit him directly in the knee. He stumbled, his great form swaying.

Tom held his breath. Would Tarrok fall? No, the Beast lurched away, barely slowing down. It was going to take more than arrows to defeat him.

How can I possibly reach the Beast's heart? I can't even get close enough to wound his knees, Tom thought, panting. He squinted at the barrel of Tarrok's body and an idea struck him. *I can grab the spikes and haul myself up on them!*

"Elenna, keep shooting and cover me!" he shouted, crouching behind a rock. Arrows flashed overhead as he tore strips of cloth from his tunic. He bound them around his hands and lower arms and knotted them tightly.

Then, with his sword at his waist, he crept behind the roaring Beast as he thrashed at Cywen and Elenna.

Tom rushed forwards and leapt at a trunk-like leg, grabbing hold of a slippery spike. He hauled himself higher, his boots sliding on the spikes, his hands grasping.

Slowly he climbed the Beast's strange body, using its ridges of green warts. As the Beast staggered about, each mighty lurch shook Tom's bones, and waves of dizziness made his head spin. Tom gripped hard and struggled on.

The heart, he kept thinking. *I must reach the heart.*

Now came the hardest part. Tom stretched out to grasp a spike on Tarrok's side. He swung himself beneath a flailing arm, and hoped he wouldn't be crushed. A few more swings and he would be on Tarrok's chest…

Tarrok drew back his arm. Tom wondered what the Beast was doing. Did he have a hidden weapon? Flinging his arm forward, Tarrok released a glob of something that looked like yellow sap. It hurtled through the air and hit Elenna in the chest. Her bow flew from her hand as she fell backwards. The sap oozed across her, spreading to make a sticky web. Elenna wriggled like an ant trapped in honey. Despite her struggles, the yellow ooze flowed across her in sticky waves.

She's going to be encased, like the three Velorans! I must act now! Tom thought.

Tom reached forwards under Tarrok's raised arm. In a few

moments, when the Beast dropped
his arm, Tom would be squashed and
suffocated. Moving fast, he grasped
a spike on the Beast's chest. Pushing
off with both feet, Tom swung around
from Tarrok's back onto his chest.

The black heart pulsed beneath the leathery skin. Tom hung onto a spike with one hand and pulled out his sword. He levelled the tip towards the heart, tightened his grip…

Tarrok's eyes swivelled, locked onto Tom. With a bellow of rage, Tarrok grasped Tom in one huge fist. Spikes pierced Tom's skin. The Beast flung Tom aside and he landed hard in the sand, the breath knocked from his lungs. Black dots filled his eyes. Through a wave of dizziness, he tried to see what was happening to Elenna.

She was still on her back, struggling with the resin. Tarrok loomed over her. A spiny arm rose into the air to crush her and Elenna screamed.

CHAPTER NINE

LAST CHANCE

Cywen swooped beneath the Beast's raised fist with a flurry of wings.

"Grab hold!" he gasped, reaching out to Elenna.

Elenna flung out an arm and Cywen grabbed it, hauling her into the air. The Beast's fist smashed down onto the empty sand where Elenna had lain. He growled with fury. Cywen's wings beat harder as

he struggled to fly and carry Elenna's
weight.

"You can do it!" Tom encouraged
him.

Elenna's dangling legs swung
towards a cactus and she jerked
them up just in time. Tarrok's sticky

sap trailed from her body as Cywen yanked her higher.

Tom turned his attention back to the Beast. Tarrok stamped his feet in the sand and sucked in a great gulp of hot air. He faced Cywen and Elenna.

"Fly to shelter!" Tom yelled, realising another sandstorm was about to blast them. Cywen tried to dodge behind a cactus, but was too slow. A wall of wind and sand hit him and Elenna with full force. Tom watched his friends tumble through the air, shrieking. Cywen's spear flew into the swirling gloom, and the gale swallowed their cries. The Beast roared again and his lumbering stride shook the ground.

There isn't time now to find Elenna and Cywen! Tom thought. *This might be my last chance to defeat Tarrok.*

Head lowered against the whirling sand, Tom ran towards the Beast. Holding the hilt of his sword with both hands, Tom put the strength of his shoulders behind a wide swing. The blade whistled through the air and *thunked* into Tarrok's ankle. The Beast roared in pain and tottered like a tree in a storm. For a sickening moment, Tom's blade lodged in the warty limb, then he yanked it free. Blood oozed from the wound, pooling around the Beast's lumpy feet. Tom leapt to one side. Tarrok staggered after him, blasting Tom with his hot breath. Tom raised his shield.

One of Tarrok's feet crashed into the shield. The kick lifted Tom from his feet and flung him backwards. His hands burned as the shield was wrenched away and spun off overhead in a blur. Tom slammed onto hard-packed sand. Pain cracked through his spine as he gasped for breath. His whirling vision darkened as the Beast's shadow loomed.

I must get up! he told himself. But he was too dizzy to stand. Instead, he clutched his sword and raised it in shaking hands. He knew it wasn't enough. To Tarrok, the sword probably looked no worse than a catcus spine.

Tarrok lifted a heavy foot, glinting with spikes.

He's going to stamp me into the ground! Tom gripped his sword tighter and stared into the twin yellow slits of the Beast's glaring eyes.

Even though he knew this was the end, Tom refused to look away.

CHAPTER TEN

FLIGHT INTO THE NIGHT

A spear flashed through the air. Its bright tip plunged into Tarrok's raised ankle. Tom glanced up as Cywen's wings stirred the hot air. The flying man's tunic was torn, covered in sand, and dark with sweat. A determined scowl creased his face.

He's braver than I expected, and his aim is true! Tom thought.

The Beast wobbled, his shadow wavering over Tom. An arrow thrummed into Tarrok's other foot. The Beast roared louder, his hot breath blasting Tom with sand. His mighty body leaned forwards. At first he seemed to topple in slow motion but then everything was happening too fast.

I'm going to be crushed!

Tom flung himself across the sand in a roll. Crouching on one knee, he hefted his sword high. He aimed the tip at the black pulse of Tarrok's heart. With a thud, Tarrok's body hit the sand and Tom's sword pierced his chest. Sand sprayed around Tom, and a great spike shaved past his face, barely missing him, and impaled its full length into the dune. Then the weight of the Beast's arm knocked Tom onto his back again and

everything went dark. Tom lay still, listening to the slowing rasp of the Beast's breathing. After a final rattle, there was silence.

Tarrok's body began to shrivel above him like paper held over a candle flame. Sap oozed away and vanished into vapour. Broken spines and papery green ash crumbled into the sand. It was hard to believe that such a mighty foe could shrivel into such a tiny heap. Tom let out an exhausted sigh of relief.

"Tom, you did it! You vanquished the Beast!" Elenna rushed forward from where she'd been shooting her arrows. She helped him to sit up. Cywen landed nearby, picked up Tom's shield, and lifted Tom to his feet. Something half-buried in the sand rang against Tom's toe.

Tom picked the object up and blew sand from it. "Look, it's Nanook's bell," he marvelled. "Kensa must have used Nanook's blood to magic strength into Tarrok." He slid the bell back into his shield.

"Two tokens won back, four still to

fight for," Elenna murmured.

Cywen shook his head. "I don't understand these Beasts—"

"Help!" a woman's voice called.

"Efflyn?" Cywen gasped.

Tom raced to the resin eggs with Elenna and Cywen at his side. The sheets of hard yellow sap were softening into sticky ooze. A young woman's head rose above the surface. Her hands struggled, trying to tear the sticky liquid away. At her side, two young men who looked identical were also fighting with the sap.

"Efflyn!" Cywen cried joyfully. He knelt to help his sister break free. Tom and Elenna leaned over the twins and pulled sap away in sticky strands, then hauled them out.

"We thought we'd died!" one of the twins exclaimed.

"Who are you?" the other one asked. "Where are your wings?"

Tom held up his hands, laughing. "You're alive and in your own kingdom. That's all you need to know right now."

He turned and gazed at Elenna. "What should we do next?" he asked. "How can we complete our work on Henkrall with the Veloran death sentence hanging over us?"

"Come back to Velora and we'll make sure your innocence is proven," Cywen urged.

"But will the Council listen to you, or to Harth?" Tom asked.

"Perhaps Pendor will vouch for us too," said Elenna.

"How do you travel though?" one of the twins asked, touching Tom's shoulders and searching for wings.

"Usually on our faithful animal companions," Tom said.

"We will carry you ourselves in thanks for saving us," the other twin said. He bent over and motioned for Tom to climb onto his back. Then he spread his wings and rose into the air. Elenna was carried by the other twin while Cywen and Efflyn flew ahead. Soon Tom could see the plateau of Velora in the sunset.

Harth has a loud voice and a rough manner, Tom worried. *I hope Cywen is right and that the Council will believe we're innocent. Otherwise, we could be flying straight back to our death sentence.*

The flying folk dropped lower and landed in the village square. There were shouts of alarm. Soldiers, led by Harth, charged forwards. Evening sun gleamed on the soldiers' spears.

"Arrest the wingless strangers!"
Harth bellowed.

Cywen, Efflyn and the twins
stepped forwards and stood in a
protective line. Other Velorans
gathered to watch the confrontation.
Tom saw several Elders, in dark blue
robes, step to the front of the crowd.
Pendor stood amongst them.

"These strangers rescued all of us
from death," Efflyn cried. Silence
fell at the sound of her voice. "The
wingless ones have saved Henkrall
from a terrible Beast that would
have destroyed everything!"

"It's not the Beast that threatens
us," cried a man. "These strangers
are the enemy!"

Tom turned to face the speaker.
He'd recognise that menacing voice
anywhere.

Igor stepped from the crowd, his robe wrinkled over his hunched back. His single eye swivelled wildly.

"Velorans," Tom said, "if we were your enemies, why would we return to you? We are friends and not foes."

"We will put it to the vote!" Pendor said, stepping forward. "All who believe the strangers are innocent, have your say!"

A roaring cheer shook the walls of shops and houses. A sea of arms waved.

"Are there any who still believe the strangers are enemies?" Pendor asked.

Only Harth folded his arms over his chest and made a grumbling noise.

Pendor ignored him and smiled at Tom and Elenna. "The people have spoken in your favour. My servant will fetch your animals."

Tom drew his sword and levelled it at Igor, who was skulking along the edge of the crowd. His hog squealed at the end of a dirty piece of string attached to a ring in its snout.

"You and your evil Mistress, Kensa, will never succeed!" Tom said. "You can tell her that her Beasts are doomed to fail!"

"On the contrary," said a silky voice. An image hovered in mid-air, just beyond the point of Tom's sword.

Kensa!

Tom stared at the witch's dark swirling cape. Her long red hair crackled as she tossed her head.

"My Beasts will triumph. You are doomed," she said. "You don't know who you are up against."

"Maybe not, but I know how to fight Beasts!" Tom yelled. The witch's

image faded. Tom shook his head
and glared at the spot where Igor had
crouched. The hunchback was gone.
Kensa's image had been a distraction
to give her minion time to escape.
Tom glanced around and saw the
witch's servant flying into the setting
sun. The faint squealing of his pig
drifted over the rooftops.

Something nudged Tom's shoulder

and he turned to see Tempest and Spark.

"Our animals!" Elenna said and ruffled Spark's fur as the wolf wagged his tail. Tom used the green jewel to heal Tempest's injured wing and the horse nickered happily and nudged Tom's shoulder again.

"You are welcome to rest here in Velora as our honoured guests," Pendor offered.

Before Tom could reply, his shield vibrated on his back. He slung it around while Elenna and the animals pressed close.

A golden line snaked across the shield's map. "A new route," Elenna whispered.

"A new Beast," Tom replied. He straightened and turned to Pendor. "Thank you for your offer but we cannot accept it. We must continue our journey."

He sprang onto Tempest's back. Elenna climbed onto Spark as the wolf howled with excitement. The crowd of spectators clapped as the two animals leapt into the air and spread their wings.

"Good people, thank you for your support," Tom yelled down to the cheering Velorans.

Beneath Tom and Elenna, the edge of the plateau streaked past. They flew out over the dark silence of the desert as the first stars pricked the sky.

At least it's cooler now and our animals are well rested, Tom thought. *I wonder if Igor is flying ahead of us to cause trouble with the next Beast. And what evil of Kensa's will we have to fight?*

Join Tom on the next stage
of the Beast Quest when he meets

BRUTUS
THE HOUND OF
HORROR

Win an exclusive
Beast Quest T-shirt and goody bag!

Tom has battled many fearsome Beasts and we want to know
which one is your favourite! Send us a drawing or painting of
your favourite Beast and tell us in 30 words why you think
it's the best.

Each month we will select **three** winners to receive
a Beast Quest T-shirt and goody bag!

Send your entry on a postcard to
BEAST QUEST COMPETITION
Orchard Books, 338 Euston Road, London NW1 3BH.

Australian readers should email:
childrens.books@hachette.com.au

New Zealand readers should write to:
Beast Quest Competition, PO Box 3255, Shortland St,
Auckland 1140, NZ or email: childrensbooks@hachette.co.nz

**Don't forget to include your name and address.
Only one entry per child.**

Good luck!

All books priced at £4.99.
Special bumper editions priced at £5.99.

Orchard Books are available from all good bookshops, or can be ordered from our website: www.orchardbooks.co.uk, or telephone 01235 827702, or fax 01235 8227703.

Series 11: THE NEW AGE
COLLECT THEM ALL!

A new land, a deadly enemy and six new Beasts
await Tom on his next adventure!

ELKO
LORD OF THE SEA

978 1 40831 841 6

TARROK
THE BLOOD SPIRE

978 1 40831 842 3

BRUTUS
THE HOUND OF HORROR

978 1 40831 843 0

FLAYMAR
THE SCORCHED BLAZE

978 1 40831 844 7

SERPIO
THE SLITHERING SHADOW

978 1 40831 845 4

TAURON
THE POUNDING FURY

978 1 40831 846 1

Meet six terrifying new Beasts!

Solak, Scourge of the Sea
Kajin the Beast Catcher
Issrilla the Creeping Menace
Vigrash the Clawed Eagle
Mirka the Ice Horse
Kama the Faceless Beast

Watch out for the next Special Bumper Edition

Join Tom on his Beast Quests
and take part in a terrifying adventure
where YOU call the shots!

FROM THE DARK,
A HERO ARISES...

Dare to enter the kingdom of Avantia.

A new evil arises in Avantia. Lord Derthsin has ordered his armies into the four corners of Avantia. If the four Beasts of Avantia can find their Chosen Riders they might have the strength to challenge Derthsin. But if they fail, the land of Avantia will be lost forever...

FIRST HERO, CHASING EVIL,
CALL TO WAR, FIRE AND FURY-
OUT NOW!

www.chroniclesofavantia.com

Read on for an exclusive extract of
CEPHALOX THE CYBER SQUID!

The Merryn's Touch

The water was up to Max's knees and still rising. Soon it would reach his waist. Then his chest. Then his face.

I'm going to die down here, he thought.

He hammered on the dome with all his strength, but the plexiglass held firm.

Then he saw something pale looming through the dark water outside the submersible. A long, silvery spike. It must be the squid-creature, with one of its weird robotic attachments. Any second now it would smash the glass and finish him off...

———

There was a crash. The sub rocked. The silver spike thrust through the broken plexiglass. More water surged in. Then the spike withdrew and the water poured in faster. Max forced his way against the torrent to the opening. If he could just squeeze through the gap...

The pressure pushed him back. He took one last deep breath, and then the water was

over his head.

He clamped his mouth shut. He struggled forwards, feeling the pressure in his lungs build.

Something gripped his arms, but it wasn't the squid's tentacle – it was a pair of hands, pulling him through the hole. The broken plexiglass scraped his sides – and then he was through.

The monster was nowhere to be seen. In the dim underwater light, he made out the face of his rescuer. It was the Merryn girl, and next to her was a large silver swordfish.

She smiled at him.

Max couldn't smile back. He'd been saved from a metal coffin, only to swap it for a watery one. The pressure of the ocean squeezed him on every side. His lungs felt as though they were bursting.

He thrashed his limbs, rising upwards.

He looked to where he thought the surface was, but saw nothing, only endless water. His cheeks puffed with the effort to hold in air. He let some of it out slowly, but it only made him want to breathe in more.

He knew he had no chance. He was too deep, he'd never make it to the surface. Soon he'd no longer be able to hold his breath. The water would swirl into his lungs and he'd die here, at the bottom of the sea. *Just like my mother*, he thought.

The Merryn girl rose up beside him, reached out and put her hands on his neck. Warmth seemed to flow from her fingers. Then the warmth turned to pain. What was happening? It got worse and worse, until he felt as if his throat was being ripped open. Was she trying to kill him?

He struggled in panic, trying to push her off. His mouth opened and water rushed in.

That was it. He was going to die.

Then he realised something – the water was cool and sweet. He sucked it down into his lungs. Nothing had ever tasted so good.

He was breathing underwater!

He put his hands to his neck and found two soft, gill-like openings where the Merryn

girl had touched him. His eyes widened in astonishment.

The girl smiled.

There was something else strange. Max found he could see more clearly. The water seemed lighter and thinner. He made out the shapes of underwater plants, rock formations and shoals of fish in the distance, which had been invisible before. And he didn't feel as if the ocean was crushing him any more.

Is this what it's like to be a Merryn? he wondered.

"I'm Lia," said the girl. "And this is Spike." She patted the swordfish on the back and it nuzzled against her.

"Hi, I'm Max." He clapped his hand to his mouth in shock. He was speaking the same strange language of sighs and whistles he'd heard the girl use when he first met her –

but now it made sense, as if he was born to speak it.

"What have you done to me?"

"Saved your life," said Lia. "You're welcome, by the way."

"Oh – don't think I'm not grateful – I am. But – you've turned me into a Merryn?"

The girl laughed. "Not exactly – but I've given you some Merryn powers. You can breath underwater, speak our language, and your senses are much stronger. Come on – we need to get away from here. The Cybersquid may come back."

In one graceful movement she slipped onto Spike's back. Max clambered on behind her.

"Hold tight," Lia said. "Spike – let's go!"

Max put his arms around the Merryn's waist. He was jerked backwards as the swordfish shot off through the water, but he managed to hold on.

———

They raced above underwater forests of gently waving fronds, and hills and valleys of rock. Max saw giant crabs scuttling over the seabed. Undersea creatures loomed up – jellyfish, an octopus, a school of dolphins – but Spike nimbly swerved round them.

"Where are we going?" Max asked.

"You'll see," Lia said over her shoulder.

"I need to find my dad," Max said. The crazy things that had happened in the last few moments had driven his father from his mind. Now it all came flooding back. Was his dad gone for good? "We have to do something! That monster's got my dad – and my dogbot too!"

"It's not the squid who wants your father. It's the Professor who's *controlling* the squid. I tried to warn you back at the city – but you wouldn't listen."

"I didn't understand you then!"

"You Breathers don't try to understand – that's your whole problem!"

"I'm trying now. What is that monster? And who is the Professor?"

"I'll explain everything when we arrive."

"Arrive where?"

The seabed suddenly fell away. A steep valley sloped down, leading way, way deeper than the ocean ridge Aquora was built on. The swordfish dived. The water grew darker.

Far below, Max saw a faint yellow glimmer. As he watched it grew bigger and brighter, until it became a vast undersea city of golden-glinting rock rushing up towards them. There were towers, spires, domes, bridges, courtyards, squares, gardens. A city as big as Aquora, and far more beautiful, at the bottom of the sea.

Max gasped in amazement. The water was dark, but the city emitted a glow of its own

– a warm phosphorescent light that spilled
from the many windows. The rock sparkled.
Orange, pink and scarlet corals and seashells
decorated the walls in intricate patterns.

"This is – amazing!" he said.

Lia turned round and smiled at him. "It's our home," she said. "Sumara!"